Quiet, Please

To Eve Merriam—SH

SIMON & SCHUSTER BOOKS FOR YOUNG READERS
Simon & Schuster Building, Rockefeller Center, 1230 Avenue of the Americas, New York, New York 10020.
Text copyright © 1993 by the Estate of Eve Merriam. Illustrations copyright © 1993 by Sheila Hamanaka.
All rights reserved including the right of reproduction in whole or in part in any form.
SIMON & SCHUSTER BOOKS FOR YOUNG READERS is a trademark of Simon & Schuster.
Designed by Lucille Chomowicz. The text of this book is set in Cloister. The illustrations were done in pastels.
Manufactured in the United States of America   10   9   8   7   6   5   4   3   2   1
Library of Congress Cataloging-in-Publication Data
Merriam, Eve.   1916–92. Quiet, please. / by Eve Merriam ; illustrated by Sheila Hamanaka.   Summary:
Text and illustrations present reflections on quiet moments in nature.   [1. Nature—Fiction.
2. Quietude—Fiction.]   I. Hamanaka, Sheila, ill.   II. Title.   PZ7.M543Sh   1993   [E]—dc20
92-44110   CIP   ISBN 0-671-79816-2

Quiet, Please

by Eve Merriam

illustrated by Sheila Hamanaka

SIMON & SCHUSTER BOOKS FOR YOUNG READERS

Published by Simon & Schuster

New York   London   Toronto   Sydney   Tokyo   Singapore

Hummingbird at the honeysuckle vine.

Ferns fluttering by the pond.

Invisible writing of butterflies.

No quack, moo, hiss, bark, howl, or meow.
Only silence from the tall giraffe.

Milkweed pods, their silky threads sprinkling the air.

A haystack in the field. The tractor wheels are still.

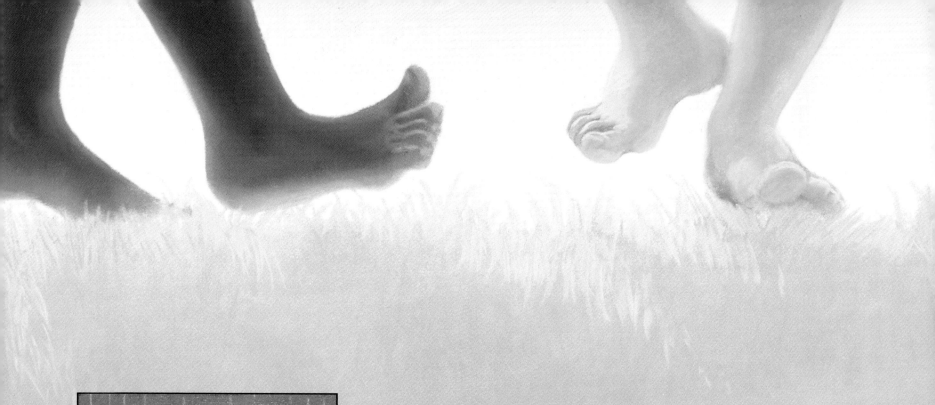

Mushrooms sprouting in the gentle rain.

Bare feet on the dewy grass at dawn.

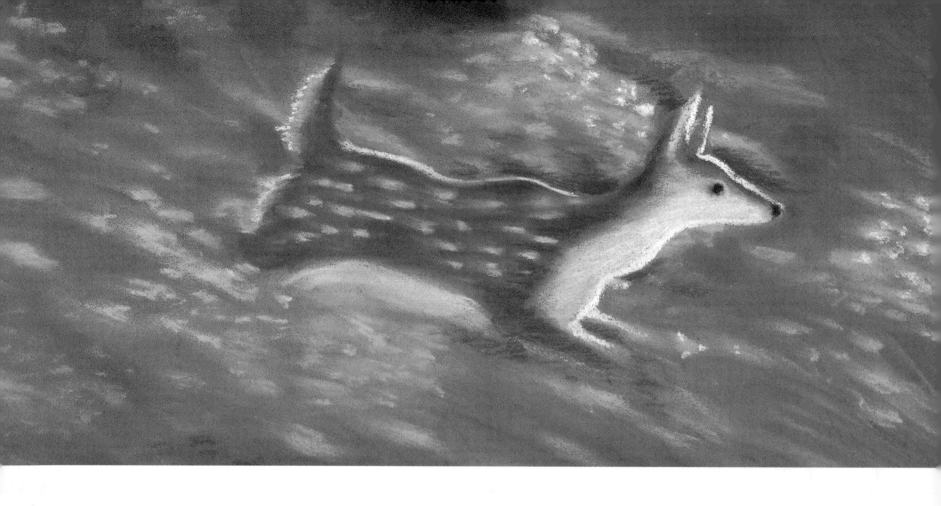

The velvet passage of a deer in the underbrush.

A golden carp amid water lilies in a blue pool.

A canoe in the early morning mist,
the paddle dipping and disappearing in dripping circles.

The bark on a birch tree uncurling.

Creamy
magnolia
leaf
dropping
to
the
ground.

Pale gray lichen making hieroglyphic
marks on a dark gray stone.

A satin-smooth piece of driftwood on the beach.

Buttermilk clouds scudding across the horizon.

A bird taking a bath in the dust, ruffling its feathers.

Blue hydrangeas nodding their flower heads by the summer porch.

Emerald moss along the path in the woods.

Iridescent bubbles of spume in the tide pool.

A tiny breeze lofting a sail.

A sponge breathing in and out.

A starfish spreading its arms.

Moonlight making a checkerboard on a brick wall.

The spider's web.

A weaver at the loom,
unfolding woolen skeins.

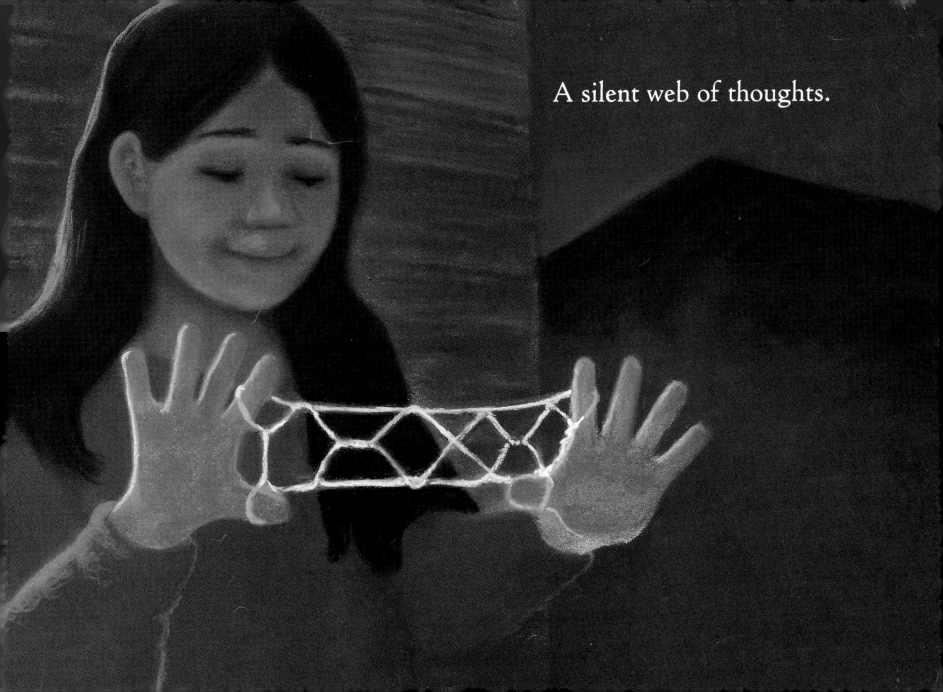

A silent web of thoughts.

The first star in the evening sky.

Snow.